Special thanks and bear hugs to Loretta Strang,
Susan Fisher, Judy Hines, Carmen Torrent, Bobbie Janikas,
Jane Jacobsen, Dottie Myers, Rosie Stubbs,
Helen Lee Fletcher, Pat Pangburn,

and

Jack Hastings, The Prince and The Pauper
Bob and Judy Carroll, Impressions West
Clara Villarosa, The Hue-man Experience
Phyllis Barton, Pictus Orbis
Mary Barrett, Passport to Adventure

Requests for permission should be sent to:

Permissions Department
Oldcastle Publishing
PO Box 1193
Escondido, CA 92033-033
(619) 489-0336

Printed on Acid-free paper
Printed in Hong Kong

ISBN 0-932529-72-0

First Edition
10 9 8 7 6 5 4 3 2 1
Library of Congress Cataloging-in-Publication Data
Curtiss, Arline B.
  In the company of bears / A.B. Curtiss ; with the polar bears of Barbara Stone.
   p. cm.
  SUMMARY: A visit to wise & magical polar bears, who teach new ways to look at time, truth, play and other aspects of life.
   ISBN 0-932529-72-0

  1. Bears–Juvenile fiction. 2. Bears–Fiction. I. Stone, Barbara E., ill. II. Title.

PZ8.3.C8785In 1994 [E]--dc20 93-86130

QBI93-689

In the Company
OF
Bears

Written by A. B. CURTISS

with
The Polar Bears of
BARBARA STONE

For my Mother, Bert Beman

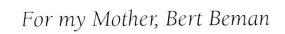

Bear Hugs!

AB Curtis

In the company of bears
There stands a MAGIC clock.
It doesn't tock or TICK
And it doesn't tick or TOCK.
But it SHOWS you have ALL the time you need
With JUST what time you've GOT.

The CLOCK was made by a wise old bear

Who measured the distance from HERE to THERE

And found IT IS ALWAYS NOW.

Still, he cannot tell you WHY

Even though he can show you HOW.

In the company of bears,

It is quite polite to GROWL

When you are not yourself,

Or turn into a TIGER cat

And LEAP right off the shelf!

BEARS don't think that you're absurd

If you pretend to be a bird.

And you can TELL them right out loud

That you MIGHT like to be a CLOUD.

HOW do you get to this place of bears?

Why, I thought you'd never ask!

It MAY be a difficult JOURNEY,

It MIGHT be a difficult TASK.

Sometimes you go by LUCK

And sometimes you go by SKILL.

But the WAY to the company of bears

Has always been UPHILL!

It's good to start out early.

Keep AWAKE! That's the DIFFICULT part.

You can't go by clock or by mile,

You have to go BY HEART.

The path of the heart is the hardest to take,

For the heart will not FOOL,

And the heart will not FAKE.

So with BEARS you can be almost ANYTHING,

A KING, a CLOWN, or a STAR.

But although you can BE it

The bears will not SEE it,

For they only see YOU who you ARE!

When you're SAD, you can sing your saddest songs.

When you're MAD, you can beat the Chinese gongs,

While the four winds moan ALL your troubles and cares.

That's why it's ALWAYS SO COMFORTABLE

In the company of bears!

You need JUST YOUR ORIGINAL FACE,

Without any pretending or fuss.

Of course you can BRING an extra one,

But with BEARS you won't use it that much.

Bears see the CROOKED and they see the TRUE.

They know PRACTICAL and MAGICAL

But they never mix the two.

To a BEAR, a kettle's a kettle.

To a BEAR, a pot is a pot.

Bears NEVER call anything something

That anything is not!

Bears have INCREDIBLE sight!
They know things are NOT what they seem,
And that BEING TRUE to your secret heart
Is the way you BECOME your DREAM!

In the company of bears
All the WORK fades into FUN.
FLOWERS spring in the dooryard,
Morning ERRANDS are run.
It is ODD how a bear does NOTHING,
Yet NOTHING is left UNDONE!

They're NEVER too busy to visit,

To take WALKS, or read you a POEM.

You ALWAYS feel RIGHT AT HOME.

When you're with a BEAR you're never alone.

You feel like a guest of honor,

When they serve you CAKES and TEA.

Bears have a way of TREATING you

so CEREMONIOUSLY!

They know SOMETHING about FOREVER

That you and I FORGOT.

While they're WAITING for us to remember,

Bears WHITTLE and DOODLE, a lot!